MW01264774

■ EASY START ■

Pat the pig's new car

"Look at my new car,"
said Pat the pig.

2

Pat the pig started the car.

He went off

down the road.

Toot, toot,

he went.

Toot, toot.

"Look at my new car."

But Pat the pig didn't
look where he was going.

Bump.

Bang.

Smoke came out of the car.

It was on fire.

"Help,"

said Pat the pig.

"My new car is on fire."

Pat the pig got out of the car.

He was very upset.

He couldn't put the fire out.

"Can you help me to
put the fire out, Sam?"
he said.

"Fill this can up with water,"
said Sam.

Pat the pig filled up the can.

"This water will put the fire out,"
said Sam.

He threw the water on the fire.

14

"Is the fire going out?"
said Pat the pig.

"Yes,"
said Sam.

"Look at my new car,"

said Pat the pig.

"What a mess."